LUCKY LEAF

By Jean Edwards

To order additional copies of this book, contact:
Xlibris
844-714-8691
www.Xlibris.com
Orders@Xlibris.com

ISBN: Softcover   978-1-6698-1158-9
        Hardcover   978-1-6698-1159-6
        EBook   978-1-6698-1157-2

Print information available on the last page

Rev. date: 02/14/2022

LUCKY LEAF

Lucky Leaf was born on a warm spring morning. He was very small at first, but with rain showers and sunshine he soon became a fullgrown maple leaf.

He loved the showers and clear warm days, and he especially loved the breezes that stirred the branches of the mother tree to which he was attached.

Lucky was on a branch of the tall green tree when the morning air stirred the branches and it felt like a dance…. back and forth moved the branches and Lucky held on tightly to his stem so he wouldn't be blown away.

The happy summer days passed and one day when Lucky was basking in the early morning sunlight he noticed his color was no longer the dark green he was accustomed to seeing - he was turning yellow. His color gradually grew yellow from point to point on his edges, and streaks of orange appeared around the veins that reached to his stem.

And then it happened!

His stem came loose from the branch that had been his home for the summer and as a gust of wind came by, away he flew.

Lucky was a little scared at first, but soon he relaxed and began to enjoy the ride.

He looked down and saw a mother duck leading her ducklings to a small pond where she could teach them to swim.

Up he flew, past the flower garden that had blossomed with bursts of color throughout the spring and summer and now Lucky was becoming tired and faded.

Over the pasture he floated where the gentle cows were grazing on the last green grass of summer.

Lucky flew on, carried by the breeze until he was over the barn where the cows slept in their stalls through the night.

Lucky flew on, carried by the breeze until he was over the barn where the cows slept in their stalls through the night.

Further on, Lucky could see woolly lambs frolicking happily in the pasture.

Lucky saw a horse in the corral and he rested on its back for a moment, then away he flew again.

He flew over a large fenced enclosure. It was a pig pen, and Lucky could see a mother pig feeding her piglets. Lucky decided that this was not a good place to stop, (too muddy).

He flew on to where the hens and chickens were eating their morning breakfast. He became stuck on the chicken wire for a moment but then a breeze pushed him free and he flew on to continue his adventure.

"What a happy life I have!," Lucky thought.

Suddenly the sky darkened and torrents of rain kept him plastered against a tree branch. When the storm was over Lucky heard the twittering of happy birds singing in the clean washed air.

Days turned into weeks and one day Lucky noticed his yellow/orange coat had turned to brown. He rested on a stone wall and surveyed his surroundings.

He began to have a strange feeling. He was tired and he began to think – "My time is about over, and I will soon fall to the earth and crumble."

"Next Spring flowers will emerge from my crumblings and someone will find my flowers and smile."

How Lucky I am to be able to bring happiness to someone because I lived!

I now realize that sometimes when things seem to be at their worst, something wonderful can happen in life.

"Yes, I really am Lucky!"

Printed in the United States
by Baker & Taylor Publisher Services